ArtScroll Youth Series®

*The greatest gift you can give your children
is the knowledge that they are never alone.*
— Rabbi Noach Orloweck

Rabbi Nosson Scherman / Rabbi Meir Zlotowitz
General Editors

Touched by a Story

FOR CHILDREN

RABBI YECHIEL SPERO

ILLUSTRATED BY SHAYA SCHONFELD

Published by
Mesorah Publications, ltd

For
Tzvi, Avromi, Efraim, Miri and Shmueli
who touch our lives every day

Contents

Heilige Hakafos	5
Car Pools and Caravans	8
A Piggyback Ride...Pretty Please	11
My Favorite Mishloach Mannos	14
Filling Up on Goodies	17
Looking for Direction	20
A Brand New Wheelchair	23
Davening and Diamonds	26
The Best Prize	28
A Mother's Wish	31
The Most Beautiful One in the World	33
Babies and Bubblegum	36
A Goody Package From Home	40
Magical Lights	43
The New Sefer HaYuch'sin	46

ARTSCROLL SERIES®

"TOUCHED BY A STORY FOR CHILDREN"
© Copyright 2004 by Mesorah Publications, Ltd.
First edition — First impression: November, 2004
Second impression: February, 2006

ALL RIGHTS RESERVED

No part of this book may be reproduced **in any form,** *photocopy, electronic media, or otherwise — even FOR PERSONAL, STUDY GROUP, OR CLASSROOM USE — without* **written** *permission from the copyright holder, except by a reviewer who wishes to quote brief passages in connection with a review written for inclusion in magazines or newspapers.*

THE RIGHTS OF THE COPYRIGHT HOLDER WILL BE STRICTLY ENFORCED.

Published by **MESORAH PUBLICATIONS, LTD.**
4401 Second Avenue / Brooklyn, NY 11232 / (718) 921-9000 / www.artscroll.com / comments@artscroll.com
Printed in Israel by Alon Print / +972-2-5388938

ISBN: 1-57819-436-9

Heilige Hakafos

As anyone who had ever seen them would say, *Hakafos* in the town of Sassov were very special. The students of Reb Moshe Leib Sassover would travel from miles around to watch the Rebbe's dancing. He would close his eyes and the entire *beis medrash* would burst out in song and clapping. The crowd of chassidim in their *shtreimlach* made a circle around Reb Moshe Leib. The "Sassover," as he was called, would speak about why Jews danced in a circle. A circle has no beginning and no end, he would say, just one flow of *Yidden,* showing that every person counts and that everyone is equal.

One year just before *Maariv,* the Rebbe was still not in shul. The chassidim wondered where he might be. Many of them figured that he was spending a few moments by himself locked in a room so he could think about the special dancing. But after a few hours the *gabbai* sent out a group of men to see what could possibly be keeping the Rebbe. They searched every place they could think of, but they still could not find him. Finally they split up into groups and began to go through the entire town of Sassov.

In a far corner of the village, one of the groups came across a small house and heard soft singing coming from inside. They peeked through the window and could not believe what they saw: There was a small child sitting in a wheelchair, and there was the Rebbe, holding hands with him and dancing back and forth. The group outside the window did not want to move — it was so special to watch. But after a few moments they walked up to the door and knocked softly.

The Rebbe stopped dancing for a moment and answered the door. He invited the group inside the simple house. Word soon got out that the Rebbe

had been found and more and more chassidim began to fill the little house. The Rebbe waited for the house to fill up and finally he spoke.

"I was on my way to *Maariv* for *Hakafos,* but I wanted to spend some time thinking about the *Hakafos*. I walked to the outskirts of our village and as I started to head back to shul I heard a child's cry. I listened and it seemed to be coming from one of the nearby houses. I walked toward it and lightly knocked on the door, but no one answered. Finally I let myself in and I saw that a young boy, perhaps 7 or 8 years old, was sitting on a bed."

The chassidim were listening to every word that their Rebbe said. By now the house was completely filled with people.

"It took me a while to calm the boy down because he was so upset. Finally, he told me that his entire family had dressed up into their nicest Yom Tov clothing and as they were about to leave for shul he had asked his mother if he could come. She did not want to hurt him, but she told him that it was too hard to *shlep* him along. He cried and cried as he told me this, and then he looked at me and said, 'I just want to be able to dance like everyone else.' Just then I looked down, and for the first time I noticed that the boy was wearing leg braces. He was crippled.

"I began to cry for this poor child. And since he was so sad I decided to dance with him and cheer him up, and that is why I was late for *Hakafos*." The little boy, Moishele, was silently listening to the Rebbe tell his story, and watching all the chassidim who were gathered in the little house.

The chassidim were silent and waited for the Rebbe to tell them what they should do next. After a few moments, when the Rebbe said no more, they began to file out, going back to the *beis medrash*. Just then the Rebbe called out, "*Rabbosai,* tonight, instead of dancing in the *beis medrash* we're going to celebrate *Hakafos* right here in this house, with my little friend Moishele."

Moishele smiled from ear to ear. Suddenly the Rebbe began to sing a *niggun*. Soon, the chassidim joined in and circles formed, one inside the other. Before long there was no more room and the dancing overflowed outside — the circles went all around the little house. And in the middle of it all stood Reb Moshe Leib of Sassov, dancing and holding a crippled young boy who no longer felt like crying.

Car Pools and Caravans

Boruch Lazerson was the "bus driver" for a group of boys in the Bucharim neighborhood of Yerushalayim. When he was young he liked the job, but as he got older, he did not like it as much and he would sometimes get upset. The boys were very noisy, and not always well-behaved. For example, when he would arrive at the school and open the door to let the boys out, they would rush out of their seats and almost knock him over on their way into school. Boruch began to think that maybe some other kind of job, like delivering groceries for a supermarket, would be much easier.

One day, he finally made his decision. He spoke to the *menahel* of the school, Rabbi Ben Shalom, and told him that he would no longer be driving the schoolbus. The principal was a kind man, and did not want Boruch to quit. So after he listened to Boruch's complaints, he offered him a raise in salary, and promised that he would speak to the boys about their behavior. But he also explained to Boruch that the boys were not really being bad, they were just being … boys.

Boruch thanked the *menahel* for his offers but said no, he had decided to quit. As he began to walk out of the door, Rabbi Ben Shalom tried one last move. "Could we at least visit Rav Ben Zion Abba Shaul before you make your final decision?" Boruch could not imagine what the important Sephardic Rav could possibly say to convince him to stay, but he agreed to see the great man.

Boruch and Rabbi Ben Shalom walked to the Rav's apartment, and sat down to talk. The Rav was a warm and understanding man. The *menahel*

explained that Boruch had done a wonderful job serving the yeshivah for the past several years and that his leaving would be a great loss. But Boruch felt that he could not do the job anymore. It was just too hard.

"If you would only realize, Boruch, that you're not driving a van," said the Rav. Boruch was confused. He *did* drive a van. The Rav smiled as he continued, "You're driving a portable *aron kodesh* and the children inside are not just a wild bunch of kids, they are living *Sifrei Torah*!" Boruch was shocked to hear this — the Rav was actually describing Boruch's job of driving the van as an act of holiness! "When you open the door to your van, Boruch, you are being honored with *pesichah*, the honor of opening the *aron kodesh*. Each child is special, each one is our future."

Boruch understood what the Rav was saying. He even felt sad that he had gotten angry at the little boys, and was a little ashamed. But the Rav said that it was normal to feel tired of driving, which is a very difficult job, and he should not feel bad about it.

The next morning the wild boys ran into the van and were met by a smiling Boruch. They were surprised at the way he was acting. "Good morning, boys. Thank you for allowing me to bring you to school to learn Torah today."

Getting out of the van, the youngest child turned to him, "Boruch, thank you." Boruch smiled, "No. Thank *you*!"

A Piggyback Ride ...Pretty Please

Reb Yaakov Tzvi Zusman was a fine young man. He lived with his family in Yerushalayim, where he worked as a *shochet*. But one day a very sad thing happened — Reb Yaakov Tzvi died. His wife, Leah, was filled with sorrow and very scared. She was a widow, all alone, and had no idea how she would be able to raise her children, little Binyamin and Uri, without her husband. Many people came to comfort Leah, and one of them was the famous *tzaddik* of Yerushalayim, Reb Aryeh Levine. He spoke very warmly to her and offered to help in any way he could. Leah was very thankful but never really believed that this very important man would be able to help her. However, the morning after she finished sitting *shivah*, Reb Aryeh knocked on her door and offered to take her two little boys to shul to say *Kaddish* in memory of their father.

Binyamin and Uri were actually excited to be going to shul with such a kind and famous man. And Reb Aryeh didn't just help out one time — in fact, every single day Reb Aryeh picked up the children early in the morning and took them to shul. And not only did he take the boys to shul, but Reb Aryeh was very kind and did not want their mother to even have to get up early to dress them and get them ready — he did that himself! Binyamin loved walking to the shul with Reb Aryeh. He would hold Reb Aryeh's hand and feel safe, knowing that someone was looking after him.

One morning Reb Aryeh was sick and could not pick up the boys. In his place he sent Reb Yoel Brand, who lived nearby, to bring the boys to shul. Reb Yoel came to the house on time and managed to get the boys out. But halfway down the street, Uri stopped and refused to walk any further. Binyamin tried

his best to convince his younger brother to move on but the little boy would just not move. Reb Yoel didn't know what to do, but he remembered that he was doing a mitzvah, so he kept trying to get the little boy to walk. He tried everything he could think of, but nothing was working. The little boy just looked down with a frown on his face and big, sad, brown eyes. Reb Yoel felt terrible but he had tried everything and Uri wouldn't even tell him what was wrong. Finally Reb Yoel cried out, "I don't understand it. You walk when Reb Aryeh comes for you. What's the problem?"

Uri looked up with tears in his eyes and said, "That's because every morning when Reb Aryeh takes me to shul he carries me on his shoulders." Reb Yoel smiled. He should have known better. Of course Reb Aryeh would have figured out how to find his way into this little boy's heart. He bent down and offered Uri a ride. It was not Reb Aryeh's piggyback ride ... but Uri took it anyway.

My Favorite Mishloach Mannos

Dr. Sergei Andropov was a famous Jewish doctor living in St. Petersburg, one of the biggest cities in Russia. He had a wife, Natasha, and a 4-year-old son, Ilya, whom he loved very much, and they were a happy family. But living in Russia was very frightening — the Russians hated the Jews, and sometimes the Russian police would just come and take Jewish men to jail for no reason at all. One night, there was a loud banging on the Andropovs' door. Usually that meant one thing — the police were coming to take someone away. Although Dr. Andropov had done nothing wrong, two men led him away while his wife and son were left standing at the door. He didn't even have a chance to say good-bye or to turn and give them one last loving look. Natasha and Ilya were terribly sad. They had no idea when he would be coming back, and they were so scared — how were they going to live? Who was going to earn money for food?

Their friends were frightened too. If they were seen talking to Natasha and Ilya, or helping them, the Russian police might arrest them as well. So all of their friends stopped talking to them and pretended they never knew them. Natasha and Ilya Andropov were all alone.

One and a half years after Dr. Andropov had been taken away, just before Purim, Ilya walked into the kitchen and asked his mother if they would be able to give *mishloach mannos* this year. Although the question surprised Natasha, she was happy that her son was interested in the mitzvah. "Of course we can." She knew what the next question would be: "But to whom are we going to send them? We don't have friends anymore." Even a boy as young

as Ilya understood that since the day his father had been taken away, none of his friends were allowed to play with him.

A twinkle sparkled through the tears that had formed in Natasha's eyes. "Ilya, we do have a friend to whom we can send *mishloach mannos*. We can send *mishloach mannos* to Hashem. He's our Friend." It sounded so simple, as if a child had spoken, but the thought was so true. Ilya too seemed excited by the idea of giving *mishloach mannos* to Hashem. He ran to the kitchen and searched through the cupboards for some food. But the only food left in the house was one stale cookie. Ilya remembered that one has to prepare two separate types of food for the mitzvah. Where would they get another one? Natasha looked at her son. "Remember how your father always used to say that we should serve Hashem only out of joy and happiness. Well, we are going to make an exception to that rule. The second item we are going to use is a cup of tears. We are going to sit down and think about your father. If we start crying, we will gather our tears in a cup and that will be our second item. I'm sure Hashem will be pleased with our gift."

Ilya and his mother sat on the floor, thinking about their father and husband and about how sad their lives had become. The tears started to flow. Together Ilya and his mother cried. And before long, they had filled the cup. Ilya's mother took the cup and placed it next to the cookie, and slowly, carefully, she started to wrap her *mishloach mannos*. Suddenly a loud knocking at the door surprised the two of them; sudden knocks on the door usually meant danger, perhaps the police. Afraid of whom she might see, Natasha slowly opened the door.

And there before her eyes stood her husband! Her heart stopped, tears ran down her cheeks, and she could not move from her place.

"Look," Ilya shouted, "look at how Hashem has sent us back *mishloach mannos*."

Ilya looked up at his mother, who was crying. But now her tears were tears of joy. Then he looked at his father. He hugged him and held onto him so tight. He didn't want to let go. Finally he looked up to Hashem and thanked Him for the best *mishloach mannos* ever.

Filling Up on Goodies

During the Second World War, the Germans forced all the Jews in Lodz to live in a small area called a ghetto. Chaim managed the apartment building in the ghetto where he and his family lived. Each morning, when people would go to their jobs, he would work in the apartment building. Wherever he went in the building, he would see if he could find a little bit of food for his family. He was always looking for bits of food so that his children wouldn't starve. The hunger was so bad that when Pesach came there was almost no reason to check for *chametz* — every home was already empty of all food.

On a very cold, wet day, Chaim saw one of the children who wandered the streets of the ghetto. This young boy caught his eye, and he invited him into his home. His name was Yitzchak and his father and mother and eleven siblings had been taken away by the Germans. The boy badly needed a home and some food. He seemed to be the same age as Chaim's 11-year-old son Yudel, but he was much thinner. He obviously had not eaten well in months.

The child had survived by hiding in a pile of garbage just outside his building when his family had been taken away. He was all alone in the world, but now, living with Chaim and his family, he had new hope. Even though they were young boys, Yudel and Yitzchak went to work every day. Yitzchak was weak and frail, but was getting stronger now that he lived with a family. He was very grateful to be friends with Yudel, who was like a big brother.

Chaim was always very proud of his son, but one morning Chaim saw a very special act of kindness. Every day Chaim would pack a small lunch for Yudel and Yitzchak. He filled each sack with whatever food he could find in

Filling Up on Goodies ❏ 17

18 ☐ TOUCHED BY A STORY FOR CHILDREN

their almost empty pantry. That particular day Chaim had made something special for the boys — he had somehow baked a piece of "bobka." Using extra potato peels, Chaim had baked a "cake."

And that morning, as Yudel's father watched the two boys from the window, he saw what Yudel did and was shocked. Yudel reached into his bag and slipped his piece of babka into Yitzchak's bag. That night, when the two boys came home, Chaim placed his hand on his son's shoulder and looked into his eyes. "Yudel, you know that I gave both you and Yitzchak a piece of babka in the morning. Why did you slip your piece into Yitzchak's bag? Don't you like it?"

Yudel looked down and apologized to his father. With two large teardrops forming in his eyes, he explained. "Don't be upset with me, father. Of course I like it. But I know that we are now living in very difficult times. And whenever I can, I think to myself that I would rather fill my *neshamah* with mitzvos than fill my stomach with babka."

Chaim couldn't believe the words he had just heard. His Yudel was the purest, kindest boy any father could have hoped for. He held Yudel tightly and whispered in his ear, "My Yudel, I'm so proud of you."

Looking for Direction

Reb Chaim Ozer Grodzenski, one of the Torah giants before World War II, usually walked home from the *beis medrash* with many of his students at his side. Even though they had just listened to his *shiur*, the students wanted to hear even more from this great Rav.

Reb Chaim Ozer lived in the city of Vilna. During the winter, Vilna was bitter cold. And when the wind would blow it would make it feel even colder. But Reb Chaim Ozer's students still walked their rebbi home each and every day. Nothing seemed to stand in their way, even when he urged them to go inside and stay warm and not to risk getting sick.

One very very cold day, while he was answering a student's question, another young man waited to ask him a question. But Reb Chaim Ozer did not recognize the second young man.

"Yes, young man, how can I help you?" Reb Chaim Ozer asked, with a number of *talmidim* on each side of him.

The young boy, no older than 15, answered, "C..c..could the R..r..r..a..b..b..i p.p.please t…t…tell m…m…me how t…to g..g..get to th…th..this str…street?" It seemed to take forever until the question finally came out. The boy had a stuttering problem, and standing nervously in front of this Torah giant had only made it worse.

"Most certainly," the rabbi answered. And even though he was only a block or so from his home, he turned around and began to walk in the opposite direction. Most of the *talmidim* had never even heard of the street the young man had asked about.

The rebbi, his students, and this young man walked through the streets of

Vilna. Ten minutes passed and the students looked at each other, wondering where exactly they were going. In the meantime, Reb Chaim Ozer walked slowly, holding onto the boy's hand as he spoke to him. Another 10 minutes passed and by now most of the boys had no idea where they were walking.

Finally, after wandering for 25 minutes out of their way, through alleyways and streets that were totally not familiar to most of them, Reb Chaim Ozer pointed to the street the boy had asked for. "Th… Th…thank y…you," the boy finally said, and ran off toward the street.

By now the *talmidim* were freezing cold. They could barely feel their fingers and toes. They were about to begin the freezing-cold walk back to R' Chaim Ozer's home, which would take them another 25 minutes. Not only that, but their rebbi, on whose shoulders rested many of the problems of Jewish people from around the world, had "wasted" almost an hour of his time. And for what? Couldn't he have simply told the directions to the young fellow? At the very worst, if the boy had lost his way he could have asked someone else.

Reb Chaim Ozer looked into the eyes of his students and then was silent for a moment. "Do you know who that was?"

They began to wonder if perhaps the boy was the son of a very important person. But then Reb Chaim Ozer explained.

"That boy had a stuttering problem. It was hard for him to get his question out, and he was very embarrassed. If I had just told him where to go, he would have had to ask again for directions and he would have become embarrassed all over again, in front of someone else. So in order to prevent the embarrassment of another Jew, I decided to walk him all the way and show him exactly where the street was."

A Brand New Wheelchair

The Bobover Rebbe, Reb Shlomo Halberstam, was a very special person. People always felt they could come to him for help and comfort in times of trouble. He always seemed to be able to find the right words to make them feel better. His smile brought warmth and joy to those who needed it most. For almost sixty years he was the one to whom many people came for help.

For most of his life, the Rebbe was a very strong man. On Simchas Torah he would dance for hours on end, holding his *Sefer Torah*. Thousands of chassidim would pile high on bleachers in the Bobover Beis Medrash, clapping and singing as they watched their beloved Rebbe dance on and on.

But now, after being ill many times, the Rebbe was weak. It was very hard for him to move around — he was in a wheelchair most of the time and he couldn't even leave his home and go out very much. Even going to the Bobover Beis Medrash, next door to his home, was too difficult for the Rebbe. He could barely move or speak.

One very hot summer day in New York, the Rebbe was expecting the arrival of his new wheelchair. Shlomo Stern, a Jewish man who owned a wheelchair company, was rushing to bring two brand-new wheelchairs, so the Rebbe could choose the one which was best for him. Shlomo drove up to the Rebbe's home and took the wheelchairs out of his truck. He rang the doorbell and was brought into the Rebbe's private room.

After Shlomo set up both wheelchairs, the Rebbe's *gabbai* lifted him up and sat him in one of the chairs. The Rebbe could not talk and could barely move, so he simply nodded to show which chair he liked more. Shlomo was working very hard and was trying to adjust each one to fit just right.

Suddenly, the Rebbe looked up at his *gabbai* and began to slowly rub his hands together. The *gabbai* thought this meant that the Rebbe wanted to wash his hands. But the Rebbe motioned that he wanted something else — a towel!

A moment later the *gabbai* returned and handed the Rebbe a towel, but the Rebbe did not dry his hands with it; instead he bent over and motioned to Shlomo to come closer. Shlomo was a little nervous — after all, he had become very sweaty and hot moving the wheelchairs around, but the Rebbe kept motioning to him. As Shlomo leaned in, the Rebbe looked at him and smiled. He then lifted up his hands and dabbed the towel against Shlomo's forehead.

Shlomo could not help but smile. The Rebbe, who could barely move, had used all of his energy to dry the sweat from this man's face. But then again, he was doing what he had always done — caring for another Jew. And the Rebbe's face was glowing, because after so many people worked so hard caring for him, he was now able to care for someone else.

Davening and Diamonds

In the great beis medrash, the *davening* had gone on for almost three hours. Little Menachem was having a hard time sitting through it all. He quietly *davened* the silent *Mussaf Shemoneh Esrei,* checked to see if his father was looking, and slipped out before *Kedushah* was said. He was just a little boy and figured that his father would not notice that he was not there. He probably had so much else on his mind. After all, his father was the Rebbe.

But Menachem was not so lucky. Immediately after *davening*, one of the chassidim came over to Menachem and told him that his father wanted to see him. Menachem ran to his father's office. As his father entered the room and sat down, he called for Menachem to come close.

"Menachem, I want to describe to you what Hashem's crown looks like." He held out his hands as if he were actually holding a crown in them, looked at where the crown would be, and began to describe it. Menachem looked at his father's hands too, and felt as if he, too, could see the crown. The Rebbe described the crown — covered with all of sorts of diamonds and jewels, shiny and beautiful. All of a sudden the Rebbe stared at his crown and seemed to notice something wrong. "Look, Menachem, do you see what I see?" Menachem looked but obviously there was nothing to see.

His father explained, "There's a jewel missing from the *Aibeshter's* crown! Do you know why? Because whenever a *Yid* answers to *Kedushah,* he places a jewel in Hashem's crown. We even say '*Keser yitnu lecha Hashem Elokeinu — A Crown is given to You, Hashem our G-d.*'"

Menachem's eyes filled with tears; he had missed his chance to add a jewel in the crown of Hashem. He was very disappointed and promised never to

walk out of *davening* again. He had surely learned his lesson. Menachem grew up … and had the chance to place many jewels in Hashem's crown — because he became a great Rebbe himself.

Davening and Diamonds ◻ 27

The Best Prize

Reb Chaim Goldfarb was a rebbi in the famous Yeshivah Eitz Chaim in Yerushalayim. Although the children in his class learned very well, he tried to get them to learn even better by offering prizes. Most of the children came from very poor homes and lived simple lives. And so they were very happy when their rebbi offered them little pieces of chocolate and other such treats.

Of course, the more they learned, the greater the prizes they were offered. If they finished a chapter in *Chumash* or Mishnah they would earn a smaller prize, but if they finished an entire *mesechta* of *Mishnayos* or a few *blatt* of *Gemara* they would be given a larger prize.

The class was filled with many smart boys who excelled in learning. But there was one child who stood out from the others. His name was Shlomo, and he mastered every word of Torah that he learned. By the time he was 7 years old, everyone thought he was the best boy in the class. His *rebbeim* had great hopes for him. Perhaps he would be one of the great Torah leaders of the next generation.

But there was something about Shlomo that bothered Rabbi Goldfarb. While the others boys in the class were excited to earn the prizes that their rebbi offered, Shlomo was only interested in one prize — money! It seemed so strange that a boy like this would want only money. Reb Chaim thought about speaking to Shlomo about his choice of prizes. He even thought about speaking to his parents, but he decided to put the matter on hold and wait awhile.

A few weeks passed and the rebbi gave a test on another *mesechta*. Sure enough, once again Shlomo did very well. The time had come for Reb Chaim to give out *sefarim* and other prizes; but once again, Shlomo asked for money instead. Reb Chaim gave Shlomo a few coins and — with a huge smile on his face — Shlomo ran out of the room. Rabbi Goldfarb was very curious about what the child would do with the money and so he followed Shlomo as he ran down the street back toward his home. But instead of heading straight home, Shlomo turned into a store.

Reb Chaim waited outside the store, as he wanted to get to the bottom of this. What toy could this boy possibly have wanted? What could be nicer than the *sefarim* his rebbi had been giving out? A few moments passed, and finally Shlomo came out of the store with what looked like some sort of toy in his hand. Shlomo looked up, saw his rebbi and quickly tried to hide what was in his hand, but it was too late. Rabbi Goldfarb stared at Shlomo with a disappointed look on his face, "Were my prizes not good enough?" he asked.

Shlomo tried to look away, but his rebbi kept on looking straight at him. Finally, left with no choice, Shlomo began to explain, "My mother does not hear well and I once heard her say that she wishes she could have a new hearing aid. So I figured that if I saved up enough money from the prizes I earned in yeshivah, I would be able to buy her one."

Reb Chaim looked closer at the "toy" that Shlomo had been holding. It was the latest model of a hearing aid! With tears in his eyes, Rabbi Goldfarb hugged Shlomo and apologized for having misjudged him.

Little Shlomo never stopped learning, and his care for others never stopped, either. He grew up to become one of the Torah giants of the next generation, Rav Shlomo Zalman Auerbach.

A Mother's Wish

An outsider might have thought that this was a very sad family. Little Ezra sat at the Shabbos table with his mother, for he did not have a father. Ezra's father had passed away a few years before. Their simple apartment had very little furniture — only two wooden chairs, a table, and the straw mats on which Ezra and his mother slept. They didn't even have a real bed.

But they were not sad. In fact, when Shabbos came and the two of them ate their small Shabbos meal, Ezra's mother felt very happy listening to her little boy talk about the Torah he had learned during the week. Ezra sang heartily and his mother smiled with joy. When the meal and the *divrei Torah* were finished, Ezra would open his *Gemara* and begin learning.

With a kerosene lamp as his only light, Ezra learned as much as he could. His mother, Leah, knew that one must not be alone if he reads on Shabbos by the light of a wick, so that he should not forget and touch the lamp to make it brighter. Ezra's mother would sit opposite him to make sure that he did not touch the lamp by accident. For many, many hours, Leah watched her son and was so proud of his learning.

One Friday night, as Leah sat watching her son, she became very tired. She even began to fall asleep. Ezra noticed that his mother had dozed off and quietly closed his *Gemara* so that she would not wake up. Since she was asleep and could not watch over him to make sure that he did not touch the lamp, he was not allowed to learn anymore. Suddenly Leah woke up. Realizing what had happened, she insisted that he go back to learning. But Ezra would not hear of it. "*Imma*, you're tired. You have to go to sleep."

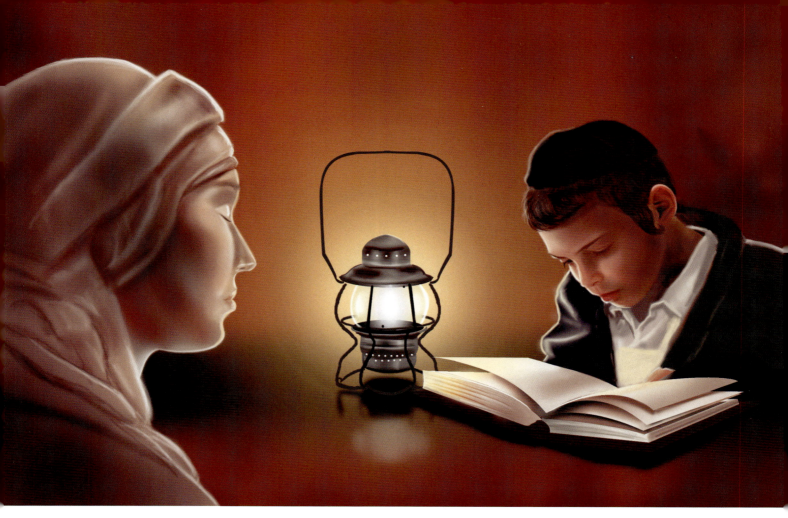

Leah looked into her son's eyes. "Ezra, I won't be able to sleep if I know that you stopped learning Torah because of me." Leah had tears in her eyes and Ezra could feel how much his mother cared for him. With a smile, he sat down at the table, looked back at his mother and continued to learn, knowing that his mother cared about his learning more than anything else in the world.

Many years later Rav Ezra Attia, one of the greatest Torah leaders of Sephardic Jewry, remembered his mother's devotion. He knew that nothing in the world would make his mother more proud than her son's learning Hashem's Torah.

The Most Beautiful One in the World

Reb Meir Chasman was looking for a perfect *esrog* — not for himself, but for his friend, Reb Shimshon Aharon Polinski, the Tefliker Rav. Reb Meir got great joy out of trying to find a special *esrog* for Reb Shimshon — this year it has taken two weeks to find the perfect one. When Reb Shimshon saw the *esrog*, his face broke out in a big smile — it was the most beautiful one he had ever seen.

Reb Shimshon thanked Reb Meir warmly and then Reb Meir delivered some more good news — his wife had given birth to a beautiful baby boy and the *bris* was to take place on the first day of Succos. Reb Meir wondered if Reb Shimshon would do him the honor of serving as the *sandek* at the upcoming *bris*. Always eager to help another Jew, Reb Shimshon gladly accepted the honor.

On Succos morning, the streets were filled with fathers and children dressed in their finest Yom Tov clothing going to shul, holding their *lulavim* and *esrogim*. The members of Reb Shimshon's shul were very excited to see and maybe even touch the perfect *esrog* they had heard so much about. Reb Meir was so proud that he had found such a beautiful *esrog* for Reb Shimshon.

Reb Shimshon walked into shul and a sense of joy filled the room. Reb Meir came over to him and Reb Shimshon wished him "mazel tov" on the upcoming *bris*. But then, much to Reb Meir's surprise, Reb Shimshon asked if he could borrow Reb Meir's *esrog*! Reb Meir looked at Reb Shimshon — why would he want to use a simple *esrog* when he had his own perfect one? But Reb Meir said nothing, and quickly handed his own *esrog* to Reb Shimshon. At that point Reb Shimshon opened his *esrog* case and removed his own *esrog* — an ordinary-

34 □ TOUCHED BY A STORY FOR CHILDREN

looking one that was bruised and had a bent *pitum*. What had happened? This was not the *esrog* that Reb Meir had picked out! This was definitely *not* the most beautiful *esrog* in the world! It possibly was not kosher at all. Many of the people in the shul began whispering and looking at each other.

"I don't understand, Reb Shimshon," said Reb Meir. "What happened to your *esrog*?! I know this is not the *esrog* I got for you."

By now a crowd had gathered, and they waited as Reb Shimshon began to speak in a quiet voice. "This morning I woke up early to say the *berachah* on my *lulav* and *esrog*. As I unwrapped the covering of the *esrog*, I felt as if I were a child in a candy store. I was so excited. But as I walked into my *succah*, I saw that my neighbor's little 6-year-old daughter was playing with her father's *esrog*. As she was passing it from one hand to the other it suddenly fell to the ground. I watched as she bent down to pick it up and saw the look on her face. She was very scared. What would her father say? She tried to bend the *esrog* back into its original shape but it was no use. The *esrog* was ruined. And then teardrops began to roll down her cheeks.

"I walked over to the scared little girl and looked into her eyes. She tried to hide the fact that she had been crying, so I pretended not to notice. I asked her if I could switch my *esrog* with hers and explained that she should tell her father that I, Rav Polinski, had found something wrong with her father's *esrog* that would make it nonkosher. But luckily, I had an *extra* one to give him. When I told her about the plan her eyes lit up and a huge smile spread across her face. She wiped her eyes and we exchanged *esrogim*."

Reb Shimshon looked up at Reb Meir and the rest of the crowd that had gathered and smiled, "I thought that I had bought the perfect *esrog*, but I was wrong." Then he held up his bruised esrog with the bent *pitum*. "*This* is the most beautiful *esrog* in the world." And who could argue?

The Most Beautiful One in the World

Babies and Bubblegum

The van pulled up quietly and one by one, the women piled into it. They were only the first group to arrive. There would be more. Twenty-one women in all. They came as their children and the rest of Yerushalayim slept. And they had come to one of the holiest places in the world — the Western Wall, the Kosel Maaravi. They came from all over Yerushalayim. Some were already in their mid- to late-40's while others were in their late 20's. But they all came for one purpose: to answer *Amen* at the Kosel Maaravi.

Standing in line at the local supermarket, Ruchi Friedman felt very strange. As the other mothers, both in front and in back of her, explained to their children why they couldn't have the chocolate and bubblegum that they wanted, she was piling those very same types of candy onto the counter.

"So I guess someone in your family is having a big birthday party," said the cashier. The woman did not know Ruchi Friedman, and she surely did not mean to hurt her, but what she said hurt Ruchi very much. You see, it was not just that it was not Ruchi's child's birthday; it was that Ruchi did not have any children of her own. Many nights, she had cried to Hashem for a child. But she had been married for seventeen long years and she and her husband still had not been blessed with one.

Last Shabbos, her husband Boruch had come home earlier than usual and had found her crying on the couch. She had tried her best to hide her tears, but now she had been "caught." Boruch felt terrible for her, and suggested that they go again for a *berachah*. He set off to visit the Stoliner Rebbe.

Boruch waited patiently to see the Rebbe. After a few moments Boruch was brought in and the Rebbe greeted him warmly and listened to his story. The Rebbe thought for a moment. He looked up and told Boruch about the *zechus* of answering *"Amen"* and *"Amen yehei shmei rabba."* And then he suggested something very unusual. "If one *yehei shmei rabba* can destroy an evil decree, then just imagine what many of them can do." Boruch did not understand what the Rebbe was talking about.

The Rebbe explained that there is nothing more precious to Hashem than the sounds of *Amen* from little children. He then told Boruch to prepare little packages of candy, and any child who would answer *Amen* loudly would be given a package after *davening*.

And so Ruchi stood in line together with all the other mothers waiting to buy her candy. After all, what was the cost of a few candies compared to the value of an extra *Amen*? Ruchi took the bag home and emptied the candy onto the table. The jellybeans and peppermint candies mixed with licorice and chocolate rumballs. With tears in her eyes she picked up two or three of each type of candy and filled the little paper bags. It took her almost an hour to make up all thirty bags.

That Erev Shabbos, Boruch walked into shul with a huge bag of candy and a few extra pieces just in case. Little notes had been given to the children in the neighborhood telling them about the candy. The *chazzan* began to say the first *Kaddish* and the congregation erupted in an *Amen yehei shmei rabba* ... The adults seemed to have been inspired by the children's excitement. The singing of *Lechah Dodi* was even more beautiful than usual. And at the end of *Maariv* the children all lined up to get their candy. Boruch reached into his bag and pulled out all the candy. He left the shul that Friday night smiling and later described the *davening* to his wife. Could a few children's *Amen's* really make a difference?

One year later the Stoliner Rebbe was invited to be the *sandek* at the Friedman baby's *bris*. After the *bris* someone asked Boruch which particular *zechus* he felt had brought about this miracle of a child. When Boruch answered that he thought it was the *Amen,* it was suggested that other people should try this plan, too. And so the chain began.

From one childless family to the next, the holy custom of bubblegum and candies was passed around. And many of these families were blessed with children.

These no-longer-childless women wished to show their thanks in some lasting way, and so they created a special group which goes to the Kosel before dawn, before their precious children get up in the morning, to answer *Amen* to each other's *berachos*. There are now twenty-one women in the group.

The rays of the sun begin to rise above the stones of the Kosel. It is almost time for these mothers to go home. Their children will soon wake up and will need to be cared for. The last one of this small group of women finishes saying the last *berachah* of *Birchos HaShachar* and the rest of the group all answer together — *Amen.*

A Goody Package From Home

Yaakov Neiman loved to learn Torah. But sadly, there was very little else in his life to be happy about. Both his mother and father had died, and at a very young age he was on his own. He was only 13 years old when he went to learn in the Lomza Yeshivah. His *rebbeim* tried to care for him and did all they could to make him happy. But there were some days when Yaakov felt lonely. He missed his mother's warmth and his father's helping hand.

The hardest day of his week was mail day. The postman would come to the yeshivah with packages and letters for the boys. Yaakov would watch sadly as one boy after another opened a letter or unwrapped a package from home. He listened to them talk about their hometowns and how their families were doing. He watched them get so excited as they unwrapped sweaters, socks and cakes — and poor Yaakov's heart would break.

One day after the mail was given out, Yaakov looked toward heaven and cried out, "Hashem, I am not complaining that others get things from home and I do not. I can live without these things." At this point Yaakov burst into tears. "But there is one thing I need, Hashem. I don't have a father on this earth, but I know that You are my Father and I am Your child. And I also want a package! But, Hashem, I don't want a package of sweaters and cookies. I beg You to send me a package of *siyata d'Shmaya,* help from Heaven, every week — help for me to learn better, to *daven* better, and to love You more!"

Yaakov was very worn-out from his tearful prayer, but when he returned to the *beis medrash* he felt something special. More than ever, he felt like he was ready to learn and to work even harder in his learning. In fact, every day that the mail and packages came, Yaakov felt as if his Father had sent him a special package

as well. Yaakov worked hard and continued to grow as a *ben Torah*. And what was best of all was the fact that he was not doing it alone. There was Someone standing right next to him every step of the way.

Many years later, when Rav Yaakov Neiman, the great Rosh Yeshivah of the Ohr Yisrael Yeshivah in Petach Tikvah, looked back at that day, he felt that his success was because of the the special "care" packages he had received.

A brave young orphan called out for help.

A loving, caring Father answered his call.

And that young boy grew up to make his Father very proud.

Magical Lights

For over seventy years, many Jewish people kept the Torah secretly in Russia. Under the Communist government it was against the law to practice Judaism. So these people, who are truly heroes, had to constantly watch to make sure that the Russian secret police, the KGB, did not catch them. The KGB was very good at finding and arresting the people who were practicing Judaism, so the Jews had to be very, very careful.

One of the most famous heroes was a man by the name of Yosef Mendelevitch. Mendelevitch had been watched by the KGB for many years. One day the KGB arrested him and put him in jail. In jail they tried to make him tell them secret information about who else was practicing Judaism. But the harder they tried, the more stubborn he became — he would not say a word. They were so angry that they put him in a jail cell by himself.

In this cell he would get very little food and would never be allowed to see the outside. He could not even speak to anyone. The KGB hoped that he would be so hungry and scared that he would tell them what they wanted to know. But they did not know Yosef. Instead of getting weaker, he got stronger. He would still not say a word.

Another amazing thing was that, even in his jail cell, with no one to talk to, Yosef was able to keep track of when the Jewish holidays were, and he knew that Chanukah was coming up in just a few days. He felt that his fight against the KGB was like the fight of the *Chashmonaim* against the Greeks. And he very much wanted to light the candles of the menorah. But how would he be able to do it?

He thought long and hard, and finally came up with a plan. He somehow

managed to get a match from one of the guards. Now all he needed was a wick and a small container of oil.

Making a wick was simple. Yosef pulled at the threads of his prison clothing and wove a few of them together. But finding oil was a problem. All alone in his cell, Yosef thought about it for a long time. Chanukah was only a few days away and he was running out of time.

The day before Chanukah, Yosef sat in his cell. He prayed for a miracle. As nighttime came Yosef was about to give up hope when he thought of an idea. Maybe he would not be able to fulfill the mitzvah to its fullest, but he would try his best and do what he could.

Yosef picked up a rock and walked over to the wall and began to carve out the image of a menorah: a base and eight stems. He took the one precious wick he had and pushed it firmly into the crack in the wall where he had carved out the form of the first light. Then he took out the match he had held onto for the past few weeks and struck it against the stone wall. Yosef put the fire next to the wick. The wick caught fire, and Yosef stood there staring at the small flickering flame that lit up the cell.

It did not burn long, perhaps only a few seconds, but the sparkling fire had lit up that dark, cold cell for a moment, and it gave hope and promise to a very brave Jew in a very lonely place.

Yosef remembered the warmth and light of that flame for a long time afterwards, and it made him feel even stronger and prouder, and determined to live as a Jew, which he finally got to do when he was allowed to leave Russia a few years later.

The New Sefer HaYuch'sin

ittle Dov watched from the hallway as his mother sat down on the rickety wooden chair and sighed. Dov's father had passed away a few months earlier, and it was hard on his mother. She worked at two different jobs just to earn enough money to pay for what she knew was most important — hiring the very best *melamdim* in town to teach her 7-year-old boy. Her home was a simple two-room wooden house. She spent money only on the most basic needs — and Dov's learning. That mattered more than anything else.

"Don't worry, Mama, everything will be all right," little Dov told his mother. And although there really wasn't much that he could do to help, when he said those words, his mother always felt just a little bit better.

Dov's mother got up early every morning to pack a lunch for him, and would then take him to shul to *daven* and say *Kaddish*. After *davening* she would take him to his rebbi, Reb Yossel, the best *melamed* in town, and then go to the first of her two jobs. During the day she would finish one job and then go to the next. Finally, toward evening, she would leave her second job and rush to pick up her little *talmid chacham*. Whenever she felt very tired, her Dov would always say, "Don't worry, Mama, everything will be all right."

One evening, after she had picked up Dov, the two of them walked down the street together. When they were almost home, they turned their corner and looked up in horror — their house was on fire. Flames were everywhere! What would they do?

Hugging her son tightly, she could hold her tears back no longer and she started to cry. Dov looked up at his mother and watched as she cried. "Don't worry, Mama, everything will be all right."

46 ◻ TOUCHED BY A STORY FOR CHILDREN

She did not want to scare her son so she quickly calmed down and spoke to him softly. "My dear Dov," she began, "I want you to know that I'm not crying for the reasons that you think. I know our house is destroyed, but that is not the saddest part. I know that Hashem will provide for us. He guards over all His children, especially the widows and orphans." Dov listened closely as he stared at his mother's tear-filled eyes. "You know, Dov," she continued, "that each night I used to read to you from a book before you went to sleep. It was a *Sefer HaYuch'sin,* a book of your ancestry. I wanted you to know where you came from and who your father, grandfather, and great-grandfathers were. It showed you who they were — and even more importantly, who you could become. And now that book is gone ... forever."

"Mama, please don't cry. Really, everything will be all right You don't have to cry over losing our *Sefer HaYuch'sin.*" She listened to Dov, but knew deep down that he was just too young to understand — he was, after all, just a little boy.

Dov stood in front of his mother, and suddenly said something she never expected. "Mama," he announced, "we might have lost our old *Sefer HaYuch'sin* but I am going to begin a new one. And my grandchildren are going to learn about me." Dov spoke like an adult. "I'm going to become the next *gadol hador!*"

Dov's mother looked into her son's eyes. She could see how much he meant every word he said. He really wanted to become the next *gadol hador.* She prayed and she hoped and her *tefillos* and tears found their way up to Hashem. And little Dov kept his promise. He grew up to become Reb Dov Ber, the Mezritcher Maggid, one of the *gedolim* of the next generation!